Duck &
Company

KATHY CAPLE

Holiday House / New York

To my Mother and Father,
who opened my first book

Reading level: 2.7

Copyright © 2007 by Kathy Caple
All Rights Reserved
Printed and Bound in China
The artwork for this book was created in pen and ink
and gouache on Arches Hot Press watercolor paper.
www.holidayhouse.com
First Edition
1 3 5 7 9 10 8 6 4 2

Library of Congress Cataloging-in-Publication Data
Caple, Kathy.
Duck and Company / Kathy Caple. — 1st ed.
p. cm.
Summary: Rat and Duck run a bookshop and work to find
the right book for each of their customers.
ISBN-13: 978-0-8234-1993-7 (hardcover)
ISBN-10: 0-8234-1993-2 (hardcover)
ISBN-13: 978-0-8234-2125-1 (paperback)
[1. Bookstores—Fiction. 2. Rats—Fiction. 3. Ducks—Fiction.]
I. Title.
PZ7.C17368Rat 2007
[E]—dc22
2006012118

Contents

1. Cat

Rat and Duck had been running
Duck & Company for as
long as anyone could remember.
"It's nine a.m.," said Duck.
Rat unlocked the door.
Then Duck hung out the sign.
The sign said:
OPEN.

"Uh-oh," said Rat.

"Here comes Cat.

Cat always gives me a hard time.

You take care of him."

Rat hid under Duck's desk.

"Hello, Cat," said Duck.

"Are you looking for anything special?"

"Rats," said Cat.

"I'm looking for a book that
   tells how to cook rats. "

"Don't you know?" asked Duck.
"Rats are not good
   for cats to eat.
   Carrots are better.
   Here is a book on carrots.
   Carrots will make your fur shine."
"Does my fur look dull?" asked Cat.

"Yes," said Duck, "very dull.
    You need this book on carrots."
"How much is it?" asked Cat.
"Twelve dollars," said Duck.
    Cat gave the money to Duck.
    Cat took the book
    and left the store.

Rat came out from under Duck's desk.

"Do carrots really make fur shinier?" Rat wanted to know.

2. Mother Hen

Squeak, squeak, squeak.

In came Mother Hen with her buggy.

It was full of eggs.

"I am waiting for my chicks to hatch,"

she said. "I need something

really good to read."

"How about *I Love You,*
   My Dumplings?" suggested Duck.
"It's not for them," said Mother Hen.
"It's for me."
   Mother Hen went to the mystery-
   and-horror shelf.

"Here is a good one," she said.
"*Terror Tales to Make Your
Feathers Pop Out.*

I need a little excitement.
It can be very boring sitting
around, waiting for eggs to hatch.
I will buy this book."

She gave the money to Rat.

Squeak, squeak, squeak.

Mother Hen pushed
the buggy out of the store.

3. The Funny Book

Badger walked into the store.

"Can I help you?" asked Duck.

"Yes," said Badger.

"I am looking for a really
funny joke book.
I take humor very seriously."

"How about this one?" asked Duck.
He picked up a book and read,
"Jokes to Die For."
"I don't think dying is anything
to joke about," said Badger.
"Okay then, how about
Jokes to Make You Merry?"
"I don't want to get married,"
said Badger.

"Here's a good joke," said Duck.
"What did the chicken
   say to the road?"
"You tell me," said Badger.

"Watch out!
   You're about
   to get run over,"
   said Duck.
"Getting run over
   is not funny,"
   said Badger.

"Don't you find anything funny?"
asked Duck.

He reached for another book.

Duck missed and fell backward
into the trash can.

"Tee, hee, har, har!
Thanks, Duck," said Badger.
"You're the funniest sight
I have ever seen.
Never mind the book now."
Badger laughed all the way
out of the store.
Duck was not one bit amused.

4. Story Hour

A stampede of little mice, frogs,
rats, bunnies, and turtles
entered the store.

"Uh-oh," said Rat.

"It's time for story hour."

"I forgot all about it," said Duck.

"Don't worry," said Rat.

"You can wing it."

Duck grabbed a few favorite books.

He sat in the story hour corner.

Duck took out the first book.

"Aren't you going to sing and play
the guitar first?" asked a mouse.

"I prefer to read a book," said Duck.

Duck opened the book.

"Once upon a time . . . ," he said.

Everyone listened.

"That was a good story," said one
of the mice when it was over.

"Now will you play the guitar?"

"I don't know how," said Duck.

"Can you play anything?"
asked a turtle.

"Watch this," said Duck.

He lay down on the floor.

"I don't get it," said a small mouse.

"I'm playing dead," said Duck.

"Ha, ha, he is a dead duck,"
said another turtle.

"Cool," said the bunnies.

"Do you know any magic tricks?"
asked a frog.
"I can make myself disappear,"
said Duck.
"No way," said a small mouse.
"Just close your eyes.
Now count backward from ten,"
said Duck.

They all closed
their eyes
and counted.

Duck tiptoed into
the storage room.

They opened their eyes.

"That Duck is amazing," said a frog.

"How did he do that?"
asked the middle-sized mouse.

"Ah, that's the oldest trick
in the book," said a turtle.

"I want to buy that book,"
said the littlest mouse.

5. Cliff-Hanger

It was the end of the day.
Rat and Duck were unpacking
a box of new books.
"Here is a new title from
the Cliff-Hanger series,"
said Duck.

Duck read the first page.
He couldn't put the book down.
"Oh dear," said Duck.
"Now I'm hooked."
Rat started to read
a copy of the book.
Soon he was hooked, too.
Duck and Rat each took a copy
home to read.

Rat and Duck got to the store
a little bit late the next morning.
Rat had circles under his eyes.
Duck's feathers stuck straight out.
"I was up all night reading,"
said Duck. "I finally finished it."
"Me too," said Rat.
"It was the best book in the whole
series," said Duck.
"You can say that again," said Rat.

Duck yawned.

Rat yawned, too.

"It's going to be a long day,"
said Rat.

Business was slow.

Click went the clock.

Hiss went the radiator.

"ZZZZZZZZ."

Duck and Rat were sound asleep.

Later, two customers walked in.

"Shhh," said one.

She put a blanket over Duck.

Then she tucked in Rat.

"The poor dears,

they've been working too hard."

The customers tiptoed out quietly.

They shut the door behind them.

When Rat and Duck finally
woke up, it was dark outside.
"Where did the day go?" asked Duck.
"I guess time just flies when you're
doing what you love," said Rat.
Rat and Duck locked the store
and started home.